# Chapter One

Mel pulled the stable door shut and looked at her beautiful Arab pony. She smiled to herself, her brown eyes shining. Candy was the best pony in the whole world! Mel had brushed her down well after the morning's lessons and now Candy's chestnut coat shone like Mel's grandma's posh dining-room table!

Mel had been in charge of Candy for a year and half now, and every day she thought how lucky she was. It was all because of Vicki. Vicki was the owner of the riding school that Mel belonged to, and Mel loved her. Vicki was everything that

Mel wanted to be when she was older: an amazing horsewoman, a good teacher, a nice person – *and* glam! Because Mel had spent so much time at the stables and had worked so hard around the yard, Vicki had given her Candy to look after as if she were her own. Mel had always loved ponies but her dad would never have been able to buy her a pony. Candy, with her velvet-soft nose and floating chestnut mane and tail, had been Mel's favourite pony from the moment she joined the riding school, so she was on cloud nine when Vicki said she could be in charge of her! They made a great team – lively Candy matched her tomboyish, sporty mistress perfectly, and it was amazing to watch them jump.

Mel jogged across to the tack room of Vicki's Riding School, where her friends were about to start their lunch. She grinned as two cute puppies scampered through the door, yapping noisily.

"Treasure! Hunt!" she shouted happily, bending down to scoop them up.

Mel had found Treasure and Hunt a year ago. She and Cara, her best friend, were taking part in a treasure hunt with their ponies for charity. Some horrible person had left the puppies to drown in the millpond. The girls had plucked them out just in time and brought them back to the stables. Vicki had looked after them ever since!

Mel was already a member of the stables when Cara joined. Cara's dad had just died and her mum thought she needed something to take her mind off it. Mel knew how Cara was feeling – *her* mum had died when she was a baby and her dad had brought up Mel and her two older brothers, Kyle and Kalvin, by himself. Cara had grown to trust Mel, and Mel had found the shy girl easy to talk to.

Pretty blonde-haired Cara couldn't have afforded her own pony either, and she'd also been given one to look after by Vicki – Taffy, a sturdy, creamy palomino Welsh. Vicki had given Cara the same talk as Mel:

"You'll be expected to muck out Taffy's stable, see to his bedding, clean his tack and prepare his food," Vicki had said, her smile showing her perfect teeth.

4

"I will, I will. Thank you so much," Cara had gasped, before running over to Mel and giving her a massive hug.

There was a group of girls the same age as Mel and Cara at the stables. They'd become friends and all 'borrowed' ponies from Vicki. There was Sam, who always stood out because of her spiky ginger hair and freckly face. She never stopped laughing and joking. Her pony, Beanz, was a skewbald New Forest cross and just as frisky as Sam!

Amber was very different. She was quiet, with big deep brown eyes. She always seemed to know what the ponies needed. She was responsible for Stella, a gentle black Highland pony with a white blaze.

Amber's best friend was lively Jess, who was the leader of the group. She was very girly and pretty, with thick brown hair and green eyes. She looked after Rose, a happy

5

grey Connemara with a gorgeous silver mane and tail.

Only one of Mel's group of friends at the stables had her own pony, and that was Darcy. It was Jess who'd got to know Darcy first. At first Mel had thought Darcy, with her very long plait, was as snooty as the other girls who kept their ponies at livery there. But she had soon changed her mind! Darcy was down to earth and nearly always joined in with the girls. Her pony, Duke, was a dark bay show-jumper. He was gorgeous!

As Mel walked into the tack room, thinking about her fab friends, she hugged the puppies to her chest. She wondered for the millionth time how anybody could have been cruel enough to hurt them.

"Oh, no, Melly, what's wrong?" asked Cara.

"Yes," agreed Sam. "You've got a face

like thunder. Don't tell me," she joked, "you've just seen Snotty Knickers. That would definitely put me off my lunch!"

"Snotty Knickers" was one of the nicknames the girls had for Henrietta Reece-Thomas, one of the livery girls at the stables. She was spoiled and rude, and the girls, especially Mel, hated her.

"No," Mel said, shaking her head. "I was just thinking about the horrible person who left these gorgeous things to drown."

"Ugh!" Cara shivered, taking Treasure off Mel and kissing his pink nose. "It makes me feel sick whenever I think about it."

"Dad was telling me about another case that he was called out to in

town about a month ago. It sounded awful," Mel told her friends.

Mel's dad was a policeman. He'd been really upset when he came home and told Mel about the young Labrador. She'd been shut up in a tiny room and was starving to death. When she'd barked in distress, the owners just threw their shoes at her. Eventually the neighbours heard the noise and reported it to the police. Mel's dad took the dog to the nearby vets so they could take care of her. The RSPCA had been called and the cruel owners were to be taken to court.

Mel told the girls all about it – she could see how shocked they were. She was so proud of her dad for giving the poor dog a new life.

"What those people did is disgusting!" Jess was almost in tears.

"I hope the owners get locked up in prison for ever!" added Sam.

The rest of the girls nodded their agreement.

They were interrupted by Vicki. "What are all these sad faces for, sweethearts?"

she asked, looking worried.

Mel quickly retold the story.

"Hmm. I remember seeing something about it in the paper," Vicki said. "Honestly, people should have to take a test before they're allowed pets. They don't realize all the hard work that goes into keeping an animal happy and safe. It makes me really cross."

"Not everybody can be as wonderful as you, Vicki," said Amber shyly. "But you're right. Some people think buying a pet is like having a toy."

"Let's not waste any more time thinking about such horrible people now," Vicki told them. "I've got good news."

"Oooh!" squealed Jess.

"Tell us, Vicki, tell us," Darcy pleaded.

Vicki smiled at the six eager faces in front of her. "I've been thinking we should try and get you involved in another competitive event. You've all improved so much over the past few months and it's good for you to push your—" She suddenly stopped, noticing Cara shaking her head and starting to go red. "It is, you know, babe. Besides, you've not even heard about the event I've got in mind. I promise it's as much up your street as it is Mel's!"

"Woo-hoo!" exclaimed Mel. "What is it, Vicki?"

"It's called a 'Pony 'n' Pooch' competition," their teacher told them.

"What's that?" asked Jess, puzzled.

"It's loads of fun," Vicki replied. "It's a jumping course, but with a difference – before you get scared, Cara! You have to jump the course twice, once on your pony and once with a dog!"

"Wicked!" Sam grinned. "Can I use Daisy?" Daisy was Sam's dog.

"I was hoping you'd want to do that."

Vicki smiled. "I thought the six of you might want to pair up. If you use Daisy, then the other two couples could use Treasure and Hunt. That way, three of you who want to jump can do that part, and the other three can run the course with the dogs. It'll be fun to train these naughty boys up too!" she said, looking at the puppies, who'd escaped and were sticking their noses into Darcy's lunch.

Mel was really excited. She loved competitions and it had been ages since they'd entered one. "Brilliant!" she said, giving Cara a hug. "I can't wait!"

"When is it, Vicki?" asked Cara, nervously chewing her nails. "We're going to need lots of practice."

"You'll be fine, sweetheart, you've got enough time. It's in the half-term holiday. Oh, and best of all – after what you were talking about earlier – it's to raise money for the animal rescue centre."

"Come on, Car," said Amber seriously. "We definitely have to do it now."

The others nodded.

"So, shall I sign you up?" Vicki asked.

The girls grinned at each other.

"YES!" they shouted.

# Chapter Two

After Vicki left the tack room, they all started talking at the same time.

"Guys, let's sit down and work this out properly," said Amber.

"You're right, smarty pants." Mel giggled. "Anyway, I'm starving. Let's talk and eat at the same time."

"Ugh!" Jess joked. "Did your dad not teach you to eat with your mouth closed!"

Mel chucked a packet of crisps from her lunch bag at Jess's head. Jess opened them, laughing. "Cheese and onion, my fave!"

The girls sat down at the big table to eat. Treasure and Hunt yapped at their feet, waiting to see which girl would give them a scrap of ham or chicken or cheese from her sandwich.

Apart from the sound of the girls and the puppies stuffing their faces, there was silence. They were hungry after the busy morning and their early start. The girls always spread out their lunches across the table and shared all their food. It was like having a big picnic every Saturday!

When the sandwiches and crisps were gone and they'd started on the fruit, Darcy spoke. "I've never heard of a Pony 'n' Pooch competition before but it sounds like loads of fun. It's good that it will help the animal rescue centre out too."

"I'm well up for it," Mel said, eating a banana. "I can't wait to do some proper jumping."

"Oh, no," moaned Cara. "That's the bit I'm dreading."

"Well, we'll pair up as normal, shall we, Car? Then I can jump and you don't have to."

Cara squeezed Mel's hand gratefully. "Thanks, babe," she whispered. "Let's use Treasure."

"Cool! So that's you two sorted. Now,

who wants to be the jumper with me?"
asked Sam.

"What!" exclaimed Jess. "I'd've thought
you'd love to jump."

"I would," Sam replied, "but you've
forgotten that we're
gonna be using Daisy.
She can go a bit mental
sometimes so I think
it's better if I go
round with her."

Darcy laughed. "I
wouldn't expect anything less from one of
your pets, Sammy! How about I go with
you and Daisy then? I'd
love to do the jumping
round."

"That leaves us,
babe. What do you
fancy doing?" Amber
asked Jess.

17

"I think I'll go round with Hunt, if that's all right," Jess answered. "I've not been jumping well and I'd like a bit more practice before I enter a competition again."

"As long as you're sure, then that's perfect." Amber grinned. "I've wanted to get back into competitions properly since I hurt my arm last year, so now I can."

With everybody happy, the girls started to plan.

"I think Vicki's leaflet said that the competition was going to be in the field behind the animal rescue centre," said Jess.

"Wicked!" Mel called out. "We can hack over before it."

"Exactly what I was thinking," replied Jess. "It's been ages since we all hacked out together."

Cara frowned. "I'm a bit worried about when we'll get time to practise."

"It'd be great to make the most of the weekends if we can," said Darcy. "It's hard for me to get back in time to practise in the week." Darcy went to a private school out of town. She belonged to a lot of after-school clubs and did prep some nights. She took really good care of Duke when she could, but her long school hours meant he had to be kept at livery.

"I wonder if Vicki will set us up a practice course," Mel said.

"You'll have to wait in line until Mills and I have finished on it." A rude voice interrupted the girls' chatting. Henrietta Reece-Thomas strolled into the tack room as if she owned the place.

"Oh, great," Sam groaned under her

19

breath. "Here comes Snotty Knickers and her only friend."

Mel got more wound up by Henrietta than any of the others. "What?" she snapped.

"Well, I mean, you lot spend so much time hanging around here. You're just like these mongrels that you should have left to die," Henrietta said, looking daggers at Treasure and Hunt. "I'm sure you can fit in around when Camilla and I want to practise."

Mel couldn't stand the way Henrietta thought she was better than everybody else. She might have rich parents, a house with loads of bedrooms and her own pony, but she was mean and nasty and, worst of all, she didn't seem to care about President, her beautiful spotty grey Appaloosa, at all. Mel couldn't understand it. She loved Candy as much as she loved her dad and her brothers. President was gorgeous *and* he'd been brought specially for Henrietta from America.

Mel scowled at the livery girl and her best friend, Camilla Worthington, her fists clenched. Camilla wasn't *as* bad as Henrietta. She wasn't as loud and in-your-face, but she cared even less for  her lovely Arab pony, Cleopatra, than Henrietta cared about President. Cleo was almost totally unschooled and wild. Over the past year there'd been quite a few times when people could have been seriously hurt because of her behaviour.

Mel was just about to tell the two snotty girls to get lost, but Amber had noticed that she was getting worked up and got in first. "Well, that's fine," she said calmly. "We'll work it out so that we can all take turns on the practice course."

Mel couldn't believe Amber could stay so cool when these two idiots were around! "That's if Vicki has time to set one up," she said impatiently. "She's well busy."

"She'll have to," Henrietta barked. "She told us that we'd be 'representing her school' if we enter. If she wants us to do well, then we need to practise whenever we want."

"*She* has a name!" Mel shouted. She hated the way they talked about Vicki. "And *Vicki* doesn't have to do anything she doesn't want to."

"I take it this means you two *are* entering the Pony 'n' Pooch competition?" Darcy interrupted.

22

"Of course," snapped Henrietta. "Why wouldn't we?"

"We're using Princess Fru-fru too," added Camilla with a smirk.

Sam laughed out loud and then quickly tried to turn it into a cough. "And, h-hmmm, what exactly is, h-hmmm, Princess Fru-fru?" she managed to say.

Camilla looked daggers at her, but carried on. "*She* is my pedigree Chihuahua. She's perfectly behaved, so with Hen and President we'll win easily."

Treasure and Hunt suddenly barked excitedly and started chasing a mouse round the tack room.

Henrietta looked at them in disgust. "I hope you don't really think you've got a chance in this competition. Especially if you're using these pathetic excuses for dogs. But then," she said snidely, "you borrow your ponies, so why not borrow your pooches from Vicki too." And she stomped out of the tack room, taking Camilla with her.

Sam broke the silence. "Well, at least the smell's gone from here now!"

Mel was flushed. They made her so angry!

Cara came up to her and gave her a hug.

"Don't let her get to you, Mel. She's only jealous because she knows that she'll never be as good as you."

"I'm sure that's not true, Car," Mel replied. "She thinks she's wonderful – she's sure that she and Camilla will win." Her brown eyes narrowed and she looked stubborn. "But she's wrong, babe, because *we're* going win. I'm going to beat her and we're going to make loads of money for the rescue centre, so that all the poor animals who are hurt by mean, nasty idiots like her and Camilla can be made better."

"Uh-oh!" joked Sam. "I don't think Henrietta knows what she's up against when she challenges Mel." Mel was very competitive.

"You bet!" Mel grinned. "This means war."

# Chapter Three

Just over a week later, Mel rushed home
from school. It was Valentine's Day, and
she'd got Candy a heart-shaped bag of
pony nuts! The girls had been training for
the competition separately over the past few
days. Vicki had said she thought they were
ready to try a practice course now and she
was going to set it up for them today. Darcy
was even going to miss her piano lesson so
they'd all get a chance to have a proper
round.

Mel charged into the house. Her dad
was still at work – he was going to pick her
up from the stables at seven o'clock on his

way home. But she could hear thumping music and the sound of Kyle on his running machine upstairs. She grinned to herself. She knew she shared her competitive, sporty streak with her two older brothers.

Mel was starving! She reached across the kitchen table to grab a banana and accidentally knocked the morning's papers and post all over the floor.

"Rubbish!" she shouted impatiently, bending down to pick them up. She started to sort them back into a neat pile, but something caught her eye. There was a big red envelope with her dad's name on the front in very girly writing. Mel got a funny feeling in her tummy all of a sudden. Had her dad been sent a Valentine's card, or was it just one of her brothers messing around? They'd done it to her last year just so they could laugh at her red face when the post came.

Mel sat down.
She knew her dad's
post was private
and she shouldn't be
doing this, but she
couldn't stop herself.
She pulled the card
out of the already
opened envelope
with shaking hands. *Dear Simon*, she read.
*Thank you for everything. What a wonderful
month it's been. Lots of love. Yours, C x.* This
definitely wasn't one of Kyle and Kalvin's
jokes. Mel knew they'd have just put *From a
secret admirer* or something. Had her dad got
a girlfriend she didn't know about?

She felt really weird. She wanted to go
upstairs and tell Kyle, but she knew he'd be
cross with her for rooting through her dad's
private things. Really, Mel just wanted to
cry. She was so used to having her dad to

herself. She loved looking after him and making him cups of tea when he was tired. If this *C* woman *was* a girlfriend, then he wouldn't need Mel any more.

Mel was late getting to the riding school. She went straight over to Candy's stable with the pony-nut heart. Candy was the only pony left there and she looked lonely. The others must have already started practising.

Candy lifted her pretty head and whinnied impatiently when she heard her mistress. Mel dropped the heart, pulled open the stable door, threw her arms around Candy's soft warm neck and burst out crying.

29

She stayed there for quite a while, breathing in Candy's lovely horsy smell.

"There you are!" said Cara from outside the stable. "I thought I'd come and check if you'd arrived—" Then she noticed that her friend had been crying. "Oh, no. What's wrong?" she asked softly.

"Oh, Car," Mel started, looking up. "I'm sorry I'm late, I—" But then everything came rushing out all at once: "Dad's got a girlfriend and he's kept it a secret. What if he doesn't tell me about it until they're getting married? And what if she's horrible? And what if he  stops loving me as much because he's got her?" Then she started crying all over again.

Candy was distressed to see Mel so upset. She tossed her head and nudged her mistress in the tummy to try and make her feel better. But it made Mel feel even worse. "See?" she said. "I can't even make my pony happy – no wonder Dad wants a girlfriend!"

"Calm down," Cara said softly. "I'll go and get you some water from Vicki's office and then we can tack Candy up together."

By the time Cara got back with the water, Mel felt a bit calmer.

"Now, start from the beginning," Cara said firmly as she led Candy out of the stable and tied her up, giving her a bucket of water and some pony nuts.

Mel grabbed a shovel that was leaning against the wall in between Taffy and Beanz's stables and started to muck out Candy's stable. Then she told Cara all about finding the card and how she felt.

At first Cara didn't say anything. Mel said, "Come on, Car. If your mum found a boyfriend, wouldn't you feel weird?"

"I was just thinking about that," she answered. "I totally would. But I wouldn't want Mum to feel lonely. If she found somebody nice, then maybe it would be OK."

Mel looked ashamed. "You're so good, and I'm so selfish," she said. "I didn't think about that. I do want Dad to be happy. I just wish he hadn't kept it a secret."

"Maybe it wasn't a good time to tell you," Cara suggested.

"Maybe," Mel agreed.

The girls finished mucking out Candy's stable, then Mel went out to brush her pony down.

"Why don't you have a good talk with your dad tonight when he picks you up?" Cara suggested calmly. "Then you can find out all about this *C* and it won't be a secret any more."

Mel knew Cara was right. If she was a nice person, she'd want her dad to be happy. He was so wonderful she could see why lots of women would want to be his girlfriend. But there was no way *she* wanted anybody to take the place of her mum. "I don't want a stepmum," she said stubbornly. "I love everything the way it is. I don't want anything to change."

"I know, hon." Cara smiled. "Just see what happens. Talk to your dad and phone me when you've spoken to him if it's not too late."

"Will do," Mel said. She quickly tacked Candy up, then put on her riding hat and forced herself to smile. "Right. If we're

going to kick Henrietta's butt in this
competition, then me crying isn't going to
help. Let's go!"

As Mel and Cara led Candy over to the
indoor school where Vicki had set up the
practice course, Mel saw that Sam had
been right about Daisy. She could "go a bit
mental" sometimes! In fact, it looked like
she was as frisky as Beanz!

"Are all your pets as noisy as you,
Sam?" Vicki laughed, her lovely grey eyes
sparkling. Daisy pulled her lead out of Sam's
hand and started chasing her own tail!

The girls smiled as they saw Mel and
Cara coming towards them.

"There you are, babe!" Vicki called. "I
was just getting worried."

"Sorry, Vicki," Mel answered quietly.

"It doesn't matter," she answered. "The
others have all been round, so you're just
in time. Though we're going to need all

the practice we can get with these naughty dogs!"

The other girls laughed.

"OK, Mel?" Sam asked. "You look a bit rough. I hope Snotty Knickers hasn't poisoned the water or something so she can beat you in the competition!"

Sam was only joking but Mel so wasn't in the mood for it. "Course not. I'm just well tired," she snapped.

The girls were shocked, but Sam didn't take offence. "Sorry, mate. Only joking," she said quickly. "Shall we carry on, Vicki?"

"Let's go for it," Vicki answered. "I think you need to get Daisy under control first!" She turned to Mel. "Are you up for your go, sweetie?" she asked softly.

"Yep, I'm fine," Mel answered quickly. She tightened Candy's girth, then mounted up and they made their way over to the start of the course.

Mel was tense, and Candy could tell. As she trotted towards the parallel bar, she didn't move as gracefully as she normally did.

Mel leaned forward to take her weight
on her thighs and knees, holding the reins
tightly. She pressed her heels into Candy's
sides more roughly than normal. Candy
flew over the bar and landed a bit clumsily,
but they cleared it.

"Try and relax, Mel," Vicki called. "You and Candy could do this course with your eyes shut." It was meant to give Mel confidence, but it just put her off. As she approached the next rail, she lost her concentration and didn't prepare for the jump. Candy knocked the bar down. It made a loud clatter as it hit the floor, startling the pony and making her shy.

Vicki could see that Mel wasn't right at all. "OK, lovelies," she called. "Let's leave it for today, shall we? I need to go and speak to Susie about the new bedding we're getting for the stables anyway."

As the girls dismounted, Mel, Darcy and Amber started to lead their ponies back over to the stables and the other girls went to collect theirs from the meadow. Vicki caught Mel's arm and whispered, "I hope you know that you can come to me if you ever need to talk about anything."

Mel shrugged her off. "Thanks, Vicki, but I'm fine. Just cross with myself for jumping so badly. I think I just need some sleep."

"OK, honey, if you're sure," Vicki replied.

Half an hour later, Candy was ready for the night. Mel felt calmer as she fastened the straps on her pony's rug. She headed for the driveway with the other girls to wait for her dad.

Cara gave her hand a squeeze. "Call me later, OK?" she said quietly. Mel smiled gratefully at her best friend.

However, her mood quickly changed

when she saw not her dad's estate car, but Kalvin's little old white one. The other girls giggled as gorgeous Kalvin got out.

"Dad phoned. He's gone out for a drink after work so you've got me tonight. Your carriage awaits, my lady," he joked.

But for once, Mel didn't find her older brother funny. She stomped across and got into the car, slamming the door without saying a word.

# Chapter Four

As Mel jogged down to the stables the
following Saturday, she thought how much
had happened over the past few days. She'd
spoken to her dad on Thursday morning.
She'd asked him about the card and the
mystery *C*, and had learned about Cathy,
the nurse at the local vets. Cathy and Mel's
dad had met just over a month ago when
he'd rescued the Labrador. Since then they'd
been out on a few dates.

Mel had been really upset and asked her
dad why he hadn't told her about Cathy
before. He had said exactly what Cara
had said to Mel the day before – that he'd

41

wanted to wait for the right time to tell her. And he wanted to see if he was going to carry on seeing Cathy before he made it into a big deal.

"And *are* you going to carry on?" Mel had shouted at him.

"I think I will. She's a nice, interesting woman and I enjoy her friendship," her dad replied calmly.

Mel scowled. "What's wrong with the friends you've already got, and me, Kyle and Kalvin?"

"Look, love," he'd said. "I'm disappointed you're being like this. You're normally so friendly and understanding. Cathy'd love to meet you and the boys. Why don't I invite her round for dinner?"

Mel hated the idea. "No!" she screamed. "I never want to meet your stupid girlfriend. Never!" And she'd stomped off to school in tears.

Her dad had been on late shifts for the past two days and Mel had gone to bed really early so she didn't have to see him.

She'd got up early to go to the stables – she wanted to spend some time with Candy. It always made her feel better. Sometimes Mel felt like she had another best friend as well as Cara – Candy!

When she reached the stable, she took her time getting Candy ready for the day. She led her outside, mixed her feed and gave her some water. Candy loved her food, and stuck her head in the bucket excitedly so she could stuff her face! Then Mel started to clean out her stable, heaving horse muck into the wheelbarrow and finding a bale of the new bedding. When Candy had finished her breakfast, Mel brushed her down, humming softly. By the time she was done, Candy's coat shone. She looked stunning and Mel felt really proud.

"Candy looks gorgeous." It was Sam, who'd just arrived. "Listen, I'm sorry if I upset you on Wednesday. I was trying to be funny. But I should learn to shut my mouth."

Mel felt really bad. Sam, Jess, Amber, Darcy and Cara were her friends. She shouldn't get in a mood with them just because things were weird at home. "No. *I'm* sorry," she said softly. "I shouldn't have snapped at you. Maybe I'm spending too much time around Henrietta and Camilla! I'm getting as bad as them," she joked.

"That would never happen," Sam said, smiling. "But *is* everything OK?"

"I don't know," Mel said. "Everything feels strange. Dad's got a new girlfriend and

I was really nasty to him about her and said I never wanted to meet her."

"Wow," said Sam. "That must be a big shock for you."

"Tell me about it," answered Mel, just as Jess, Amber and Cara turned up.

"Morning, guys!" called Jess. Then she saw their serious faces and said, "Sorry. Is this a private chat?"

Mel shook her head. "No. And I'm sorry for being so moody." And she filled them all in, starting with finding the Valentine card.

When she'd finished, Jess put an arm round her. "I know how you feel," she said. "Last year my mum went out on a date with somebody from work and I hated it. It made me feel really horrible."

"I know it's easy for me to say," said Amber softly, "but maybe you *should* meet Cathy. It's a weird thing to get used to, but she might turn out to be really nice and it sounds like your dad would be pleased if you did."

"I think so too," agreed Cara. "Why don't you give it a go?"

As the others got their ponies ready for the morning's work, they gossiped and chatted, but Mel was quiet as she tacked Candy up. She thought hard about what her friends had said. Her dad had brought her up by himself and he'd always been there, no matter what. She didn't want to share him with anybody, but now it was her turn to be there for him.

"You're right, guys," she said to them as they all led their ponies over to the outdoor school, where the first class of children was waiting. "I'll tell Dad I'm sorry."

"Good one, babe," Jess said. "I know you'll feel better when you and your dad make friends again."

Mel didn't have any time to think about her dad or Cathy during the morning. Just a month ago, the school had been used in an episode of a famous TV soap, and since then it had been really popular. Vicki had taken on quite a few more pupils and had had to add an extra lesson on a Saturday morning.

By one o'clock all the girls and ponies were shattered! Mel and the other yard girls led their ponies back to the stables and quickly untacked them and brushed them down. When they'd given them hay and water, they walked over to the tack room to have their own lunch.

Darcy was waiting for them. "Hey, guys! Good morning?" she asked.

"Yes," Amber answered. "Some of the

new Saturday kids are really good. Vicki's pleased with them. How about you?"

"Yes, good, thanks," she answered. "I'm well looking forward to the competition! When am I going to meet Daisy, Sam?"

"Well, actually," Sam replied, "I've been working with her at home and she's getting loads better. Mum's dropping her off after lunch so we can do another proper practice round."

"Hmmm," Amber said, looking thoughtful. "I heard Henrietta and Camilla planning to use the course straight after lunch."

"Oh, Henrietta's such a pain!" Jess moaned. "I know it's a bit mean, but I wish she'd leave the stables. She spoils everything."

"It's not mean," Mel exclaimed. "She knew we wanted to use the course this afternoon – she heard me and Cara talking about it when we were mucking out President yesterday."

"Oh, well," Cara said, trying to calm her friend down. "We can work with the puppies first. They're still so naughty, it's probably best anyway. You and Candy hardly need any practice anyway."

An hour later, the girls had arranged some pieces of piping in the yard for the dogs to get used to jumping over. Sam's mum dropped Daisy off and they soon began to see that Cara was right! Hunt kept climbing inside the pipe instead of jumping over it and Treasure kept trying to bite Cara's heels – and as for Daisy! Her concentration was about as good as her mistress's! She'd tackle one jump perfectly and then get distracted and start running around, barking wildly.

"Oh, no!" Mel said. "We have to beat

Toffee Nose, but we don't know anything
about dog training."

"Maybe we need to be stricter with
them," Darcy wondered.

"We should ask Vicki for some help,"
Amber suggested.

"Good idea, babe," came Vicki's voice
from across the yard. She scooped up Daisy,
who was just about to start digging in the
muck heap, and walked over to the girls.

51

"Henrietta and Camilla have just finished. Shall I stay here with you three?" she asked Sam, Jess and Cara. "We need to get these dogs obeying your voices. You three," she said to Darcy, Amber and Mel, "could go and do some jumping work with Susie."

"Cool!" cried Mel enthusiastically. "Let's do it!"

"Listen, Mel, don't take it too seriously," Vicki warned. "I know it's a competition but it is supposed to be fun."

"I know. I'm sorry," Mel said, looking at the floor. She hated it when Vicki told her off.

But Vicki grinned and winked. "Anyway, between you and me, babe, you've got absolutely nothing to worry about!"

# Chapter Five

The next day, Mel was starting to panic. She *did* have something to worry about. The jumping just wasn't going as well as normal and the competition was in two days' time! And Candy seemed as tired and grumpy as she was.

"Argh!" she shouted as Candy knocked the same jump down for the fourth time. "This should be well easy, but I can't get it right. Car, we might have to swap so you can do the jumping."

"Don't even joke. I couldn't," said Cara seriously, getting stressed out just thinking about it.

"Who said anything about joking?" Mel asked. "What's wrong with me? Why can't I do this any more?"

"You've got loads on your mind. Don't worry – on the actual day you'll be wicked as usual."

"OK. Let's try again for a clear round from all of us," Mel said, trying to get into the mood. "I need a rest, so why don't you and Treasure go first?"

Mel and Candy trotted back to the start line, where Vicki stood smiling.

"Come on, babe, calm down. You can do this."

"I wish," Mel said crossly.

Cara was still trying to help Mel and didn't let her own nerves show. She'd worked hard with Treasure all morning. He was naughtier than Hunt but was improving loads. Cara had taught him to obey her using lots of doggie treats and hugs, and now he could do a clear round nearly every time.

"Good one, Car!" Mel shouted as Cara and Treasure reached the end. "I won't let you down." Clearing her head of everything except the course, she leaned forward in the saddle and Candy took the first jump perfectly. She did the same with the second and third jumps. Vicki and Cara whooped.

"I told you, Mel," Cara shouted. "We're so going to beat Henrietta!"

Mel only had two more jumps to go. Stupidly, she started to let her mind wander. *I wonder if Dad will come and watch?* she thought. For a moment she'd forgotten that she was meeting Cathy that evening. As she remembered, she tensed up: Candy felt it immediately, missed her stride, and the bar clattered down, while Mel landed in a heap on the ground. Vicki ran over to grab Candy before she bolted.

Treasure was startled by the noise and

barked loudly. He pulled his lead out of Cara's hand and dashed over to the rest of the girls, who were waiting in the practice ring.

Then Henrietta and Camilla arrived too!

Henrietta's nasty laugh rang out around the indoor school. "Well," she sniggered, "it doesn't look like we've got *anything* to worry about. You idiots look worse, not better."

"Uh-oh," whispered Sam to Darcy. "Mel's gonna give it to her now."

But to their surprise, Mel simply burst into tears.

Henrietta wasn't sympathetic. "There's no need to be a baby about falling off."

"That's enough, Henrietta," snapped Vicki. "Darcy and Sam are next. Can you both please leave till it's your turn?"

"Oh, Vicki," Camilla whinged. "We wanted to go next so we could get home. We've been working really hard all day."

Jess sniggered at the thought of the lazy livery girls working hard, but Vicki didn't find it funny at all. Her eyes flashed dangerously as she passed Candy's reins to Cara.

"I said, *leave*," she said firmly as she helped Mel to her feet. "Are you hurt?" she asked.

Mel just shook her head.

"Good. Now listen to me, Mel," Vicki went on. "You will be fabulous in this competition, you just need to concentrate. I don't think you should do any more practice at all."

Mel started to argue and Cara stuttered nervously, but Vicki cut them both off. "No, I'm serious. It's doing more harm than good. Why don't you both go and spend some quality time with your ponies? Mel, Candy looks as tired as you. And Cara, Taffy's hardly seen you because you've been practising so hard with the dogs. Go."

Vicki was right, Mel thought later as she brushed the last bits of straw and mud off Candy's coat and mane. She was already feeling calmer and Candy seemed less grumpy too.

Soon she heard her friends outside in the yard. She went over to Stella's stable. "I'm sorry for being such a wuss before, Am," she said.

"Babe, you're having a rubbish time at the moment – who cares what stupid Snotty Knickers says? She's not important," Amber replied.

"I know," Mel said. "I just *so* want to to wipe that silly smile off her face on Tuesday."

"It's not the end of the world if you don't, you know," Amber said sensibly.

Sam and Jess joined them. "You never know," Sam joked. "Daisy might decide to behave for once in her life. If you don't feel like beating Henrietta in the Pony 'n' Pooch, maybe we could do it for you!"

The girls laughed, but Jess put her arm round Mel. "How's everything with your dad and stuff?" she asked softly.

"OK," Mel said. "I'm meeting Cathy tonight. She's coming over for dinner.

Maybe I'll feel better when that's over with.
And then I'll be brilliant on Tuesday!"

"You bet!" Jess answered.

"Yep, you're our star jumper," Sam
whooped.

Mel wasn't sure she was a star anything
later that evening. She had promised her
dad and herself that she'd be nice to Cathy
– Kyle and Kalvin both were – but she just
couldn't do it. Cathy wasn't even pretty.

She had plain mousy-coloured hair and plain, boring clothes. Mel couldn't help comparing her to Vicki, who looked glam no matter what she was doing or what she was wearing.

"So, what's your favourite subject at school?" Cathy asked her, trying to be friendly. "From what your dad's been saying, it must be PE!"

Before she could stop herself, Mel answered moodily, "If you know already, then why bother to ask?"

"That's enough, Melanie," her dad snapped. "If you can't be polite, go and eat in your room."

"Fine. I don't want to be here anyway—" she started.

The phone rang suddenly, interrupting them. Her dad got up to answer. "I'm not on call," he said crossly. "I wonder who it is."

"Phew! Saved by the bell." Cathy smiled sympathetically.

Mel said nothing. Her dad was using his serious voice. It must be work.

"Oh, no . . . OK . . . And how serious is that? . . . What can I do? . . . Yes, of course," he was saying.

When her dad came back, he looked very grave and his voice was completely different.

"Sit down a minute, Mel," he said firmly.

Thinking she was going to be told off, she started to argue. "No, Dad, it's—"

"No, Mel. *Sit down*," he insisted, then reached out and took her hand. "Melly," he said softly, "that was Vicki. When she went to do her evening check-up on the ponies, she found Candy in quite a lot of distress. She's really not well and Vicki's going to have to call out the emergency vet."

Mel gasped and tears came into her eyes. "What's wrong?" she cried.

"Vicki's not sure. She's got strange swellings that Vicki's never seen before."

"I need to see her," Mel shouted, getting worked up.

"I could come with you," Cathy interrupted. "I might be able to help while we wait for the vet."

"No!" Mel snapped. "I don't want you near my pony."

"Mel," her dad said. "Surely you want what's best for Candy? Cathy might be able to help. We'll all go."

# Chapter Six

Mel was sobbing as she grabbed her coat and trainers from the hall. When she came back, Cathy was on the phone to Vicki.

"Yes . . . Sounds like an allergic reaction . . I'll come and see if I can help. Jo, from my surgery, should be at home and might be able to come quicker. In the meantime, can you think if anything in Candy's diet or environment has changed recently?" She put down the phone and grabbed her own coat from the back of the chair.

"OK," she said softly. "It sounds like Candy's had an allergic reaction to something. The on-call vet is out on an emergency on the other side of town and could be a while. If I come with you now, I should be able to help calm Candy down."

"What does she need to make her better?" asked Mel.

"If it is a simple allergic reaction, then an injection should do it," Cathy answered. "I'll call Jo, my boss, and see if she minds coming out – she'll have Candy sorted in no time. Don't panic."

But Mel *was* panicking. The thought of Candy in pain made her feel sick. What if she died? Mel didn't know what she'd do.

Vicki was waiting for them at the top of the driveway when they arrived.

"Is she OK? Is she OK?" Mel gasped.

"I think so, darling. Don't get too upset when you see her. She doesn't look like her normal beautiful self. She's got swellings on her face and legs," Vicki said. "Don't worry though. I promise we'll get her sorted."

"Where is she?" Cathy asked, getting out of the car.

"Follow me," Vicki said. They rushed over to the stables.

Mel gasped when she saw Candy. She was tossing her head and whinnying in distress. Her head and neck had lots of angry-looking lumps on them and her eyelids and lips were swollen. From her knees and hocks downwards she had horrid lumps that looked really sore and itchy.

Mel was so upset she burst into tears.

Her dad put his arm round her. "Come on," he said soothingly. "We'll make her better."

"Yes, we will," Cathy said calmly. "Now, Simon, if you keep calling Jo till she picks up, then I can concentrate on helping Candy till she gets here." She rolled up her sleeves and scraped her mousy hair back into a ponytail. "This definitely looks like an allergic reaction, honey," she said to Mel.

Then she turned to Vicki. "These hives on her head and lower limbs will be itchy and hot," she said. "We need to cool her down and stop the itching or she's going to start getting really distressed. Is there a bucket and sponge so we can bathe her?"

"Course, I'll get them," called Vicki over her shoulder, already running off towards the tack room.

As Vicki left, Mel spoke. "What could she be allergic to?" she asked. "It looks so horrible. Has she been poisoned?"

"No. Nothing like that," Cathy answered. "It could be any little thing you've changed over the past few days. Can you think of anything? Any different food? Shampoo? Bedding?"

"Yes! Bedding!" Mel answered quickly, remembering the new bale of straw she'd opened the day before. "I don't know what it is now or when it changed. It doesn't look any different," she told Cathy in a rush. "Could it be that?"

"Definitely possible," Cathy replied just as Vicki ran back with the bucket.

Mel's dad followed too. "I've just got through to Jo. She needs to speak to you, Cathy."

"Hi, Jo. Change of plan," Cathy said quickly down the phone. "She's a five-year-old Arab – a beauty."

Mel felt proud when she heard Cathy say this. But as she looked over at her pony, she panicked. Candy didn't look beautiful now. What if she never recovered?

Mel didn't understand half the words
Cathy was using to speak to Jo. "Her head
and lower limbs are covered in urticaria.
Obvious cause is a change in bedding over
the past couple of days." She paused for a
second and looked up at Vicki, raising her
eyebrows.

Vicki hit her hand against her head. "Of
course," she said, annoyed with herself.

"How could I have been so stupid?"

"Yes," Cathy repeated. "Change in bedding. Came on suddenly. Acute. Looks like she needs a high-dose antihistamine shot. Do you have any in your bag?" She stopped, looked over at Mel and smiled reassuringly. "You have? . . . Brilliant. Any chance you could come over? I think Phoebe's on call tonight and she's already out on an emergency . . . Great, see you then," she said, hanging up. "OK," she told Mel and Vicki. "Jo's on her way over. Let's get Candy as comfy as possible till she gets here. We need to move her out of this stable and get her cooled down. This bedding will just keep irritating her otherwise."

Vicki led Candy out into the yard and spoke softly to Mel. "Mel, honey, let's get Candy's stable mucked and swept out. There's still some of the old bedding left on the left-hand side of the barn."

Mel started sweeping out Candy's stable straight away, watching Cathy and Vicki closely all the while. Vicki was sponging Candy down with cold water and Cathy was speaking softly to the pony. "You're a brave girl," she was saying. "And beautiful. We'll soon have you sorted." And Candy *was* calming down a bit.

Mel's dad came over to join his daughter in the stable. He had a yard brush in his hand. "I'm feeling a bit useless, just watching you girls make Candy better. Let your old dad give you a hand, hey, Mel?" he said, trying to cheer her up.

Mel said nothing. She felt useless too. She wished she could help Cathy and Vicky. She was scared and her heart was pounding in her chest.

She looked up at her dad. She didn't want to speak in case she cried, so they mucked out together in silence. When it was done, Mel filled up Candy's water bucket and swilled the stable out before going to get some of the old straw as Vicki had instructed.

Twenty minutes later, Cathy came into the clean stable to say that Jo had arrived. They went out into the yard and watched as the vet put on her gloves, took a needle

out of a secure box and gave Candy an
injection.

"Thank you so much for coming out,"
Vicki said to her as she took off her gloves.

"No problem. Glad I could help,"
Jo answered. Then she turned to Cathy.
"Are you OK to finish off here, Cath?" she
asked. "Just needs lots of fluid and tucking
up for the night, I think."

"Course," Cathy answered, smiling.
"Thanks again, Jo. See you in the morning."

"I'll walk you to your car," Vicki said to the vet, and they headed out of the yard.

Mel chased after them. "Thank you so much," she said to Jo.

"You're welcome, sweetheart," she answered, smiling at the worried girl. "I'm sure she'll be fine, but I'll pop back in the morning and check up on her."

"Thank you," Mel said again.

"I did the easy bit really, you know. It was Cathy who diagnosed her and kept her calm," Jo said, and went across to her car.

Mel looked over at Cathy. She was leading Candy back into her clean stable. The pony looked a bit better already. She was definitely calmer and the lumps on her head didn't look as bad. She walked slowly up to Cathy, who was now talking softly to Mel's dad outside Candy's stable.

"Thank you, Cathy," she said.

# Chapter Seven

Mel jogged back to the stables early the next morning. She was so glad it was half term. It meant she didn't have to rush off to school once she'd checked on Candy. It had been a late night, and she'd hardly slept because she was still so worried.

When she ran up to Candy's stable, Vicki was already there, sponging the pony down again.

"How is she?" Mel gasped, panting for breath.

"She's fine, babe. Jo's already been and given her the once over and says she just needs another day to rest. It's a good job

Cathy was around when I called. I was just so upset by how bad Candy looked. I didn't think it could be anything as simple as an allergic reaction. Some can be really serious if they're left, but getting the straw out and that injection seems to have done the trick."

"So was it her bedding then?" Mel asked.

"It must have been. I've not changed anything else. I only changed the bedding supplier because so many deliveries were late. I've called this morning and changed it back though. I'd rather have it late than hurting my precious ponies."

"It's so weird to think that ponies can get allergic reactions just like we can," Mel said.

"I know," Vicki answered with a smile. "Candy's still swollen and obviously tired, but she's a tough girl. The vet says by tomorrow she'll be able to do the Pony 'n' Pooch competition as long as you take it easy. The exercise might do her good actually."

Mel had totally forgotten about the competition. Making sure that Candy was OK had been the only thing on her mind. Now she was so relieved that she was suddenly exhausted. So much had happened over the past week!

"I take it Cathy is the reason you've been finding things so difficult?" Vicki asked.

Mel took a deep breath, and then told Vicki everything as the two of them carried on sponging Candy down. "I don't know, Vicki. I mean, she saved Candy's life. I know I should be nice to her but I just can't," she finished.

Vicki stopped sponging. "Babe," she said

calmly, "you have to give this woman a chance. We couldn't have done without her last night. She rushed out here on her evening off to help us and Candy out." She stopped and looked at Mel. "She does seem very nice. I can't tell you what to do, but I'd like to think that you were a big enough person to give her a chance, *especially* after what she did last night."

Mel didn't get a chance to answer. At that moment the rest of her friends arrived, gossiping loudly.

Vicki smiled at her. "I'll let you fill the girls in on what's been going on round here, Mel," she said. "Then the rest of us can all get some practice in. You two though," she said firmly, pointing to Mel and Candy, "need a rest."

"What's going on?" asked Jess, concerned. "Is everything OK?"

As Vicki walked off, taking the bucket and sponge with her, Amber noticed Candy.

She still had some ugly bumps on her head and legs and was definitely not her normal lively self. "Gosh!" she cried. "What *has* been going on?"

Mel filled them in on her night-time adventure.

When she'd finished, Darcy said, "Wow, Mel. Cathy sounds like a hero."

Mel nodded. "She was, I suppose. Candy looked so awful last night, even Vicki didn't know what to do. But Cathy was really calm and got it all sorted and Candy's

81

gonna be fine," she finished, giving her pony a hug.

"She does sound like a nice lady, Mel," Jess agreed.

"You know what? I think she is. Now Candy needs a rest, so I'm going to come and cheer you all on while you practise." Mel grinned at her friends.

"You'll have to cheer *us* on first," Henrietta said, passing by on her way to President's stable.

"You probably need all the practice and cheering you can get – but no way, sorry," Mel answered.

"Oh, look," Henrietta said nastily to Camilla. "Mel can't have fallen off yet today – she's still cocky."

Mel knew that Candy wasn't fit enough to win the Pony 'n' Pooch competition now, but if she couldn't wipe that smug smile off Henrietta's face herself, then she was going to make sure that one of her friends did! "Come on, girls," she shouted. "Let's practise till we know we can get first, second and third place in this competition!"

By the next morning Candy's swellings had gone down completely. There were a few marks left where the lumps on her head had been, but she was more like herself again. She lifted her lovely head when she heard Mel's footsteps and whinnied softly.

Mel spent a long time getting her pony ready for the competition – the least she could do was make her look as gorgeous as possible. She was concentrating so hard on what she was doing that she didn't hear any of the other girls arrive, so it was a big surprise when Vicki came over.

"Right, girls," she said. "Let's get ready to hack over, shall we?"

"Yey!" said Jess excitedly. She looked really pretty in her smartest riding clothes.

Vicki handed them their entry numbers to pin on their backs and went off to get Jelly, her fabulous Irish-cross thoroughbred, while the girls tacked up ready to set off.

# Chapter Eight

They had a very chilled-out hack over and
arrived with lots of time to spare. The field
was heaving with people.

"Gosh!" Vicki cried as they waited at the
edge of the field. "What a good turnout!"

"Oh, no," mumbled Cara. "I didn't realize there'd be so many people taking part. I'm not sure Treasure and me are good enough yet."

"Come on, Car," Jess said enthusiastically. "It'll be well good. There's a wicked atmosphere."

"Yeah," Mel said, smiling reassuringly at her best friend. "You and Treasure have been amazing in practice. Loads better than Candy and me. Anyway, it's only a bit of fun, isn't it?" She grinned over at Vicki.

"You'll have a great time no matter where you end up coming," Vicki answered. "Anyway, the main thing is that you girls do your best. You always make me really proud."

The girls blushed happily. They idolized Vicki, so when she praised them like this they felt very happy!

"Ah, look," Amber called. "Susie and the

puppies are here." Susie had driven Treasure
and Hunt over in Vicki's old Jeep.

"Good," said Vicki, spotting Susie pulling
into the car park. "Before she brings them

over, let's get these ponies sorted. Jess, Sam
and Cara, you bring your ponies with me
and Jelly. The ponies that aren't competing
are staying in the meadow on the other side
of the field."

"Will they be OK?" worried Cara.

"They'll have a great time messing
around while we do all the hard work!"
Vicki laughed. "Now stop worrying and let's
go. You other three are probably best just
staying here."

 By the time Jess,
Sam and Cara
had arrived back
with Vicki, Susie
had made her
way over with
Treasure and
Hunt on their
leads, and Sam's

mum and Daisy had arrived too.

Mel and Cara started looking at the gathering crowd to see who had arrived. Mel wanted to check if her dad was there yet. He was working, but he'd said he was going to take his break early so he could come and see Mel and Candy in action. Mel smiled when she thought how different Candy looked from the last time he'd seen her.

"Ugh," Cara said. "There's Mr Reece-Thomas." The rest of the girls all turned to see the horrible man. He was standing talking to a tall woman, who was looking down her big pointy nose.

"Well, we know who she's got to be!" laughed Darcy.

"Who?" asked Sam, who was trying to stop Daisy from chewing Jess's riding boot.

"Look," Darcy answered, smiling. "You'll know for sure."

"Uh-oh," Sam answered with a groan. "It has to be Camilla's mum. She looks well like her."

"That means she and Toffee Nose have arrived too," Mel said. "We'll probably hear them any second."

"There's your mum and brother, Jess," Darcy called. "Oh, and a couple of rows behind are Mum and Dad and Belle, with your mum, Car."

"Oh, no," Cara whispered. "I love it that Mum comes to watch me in stuff, but it makes me even more nervous. I don't think I can do it."

"We'll be fine, Car," Mel said reassuringly. "Don't worry, I won't let you down—" She broke off suddenly. She'd spotted her dad in the crowd. He was in his policeman's uniform and looked really smart. And next to him . . . was Cathy!

"Hold Candy for me, would you?" she asked, shoving Candy's reins into Cara's hand. She rushed over and threw her arms round her dad. "I'm sorry, Dad. I've been so mean. I'm glad you're here."

"Well, I'm glad too, love. I know it's been hard for you and I should have been honest with you from the start. It takes a big person to say they're sorry. I'm proud of you."

Mel blushed and took a deep breath. She turned to Cathy. "I'm really sorry for treating you so badly. I was rude and you didn't deserve it – and thank you so much for helping Candy like you did," she finished quickly, her heart beating fast.

"Thank you, Mel. It means a lot that you'd say that. I'm glad I was there to help Candy. She's really beautiful," Cathy said, smiling at Mel's flushed face. "Just like her mistress."

Mel grinned back, then hugged her dad again, just as a man's voice called through a microphone, *"Could all contestants kindly make their way to the starting area? The Pony 'n' Pooch competition will begin in five minutes' time."*

"I'd better go," Mel said shyly.

"OK," answered her dad. "Kyle and Kalvin should have arrived and they'll be watching somewhere in the crowd, but take it easy. You and Candy have both had a hard week."

"Good luck!" Cathy called.

# Chapter Nine

Sam and Darcy were the first contestants. And they were brilliant! Every time Mel watched Darcy and Duke together, she felt a bit jealous. They were really smooth and graceful. Darcy judged the jumps perfectly, making sure that Duke met each one just right. They were very quick

and didn't get any faults at all!

Surprisingly, Sam and Daisy were just as good! Daisy behaved perfectly, as though she was the most well-behaved dog in the world!

Sam was fit and liked sport nearly as much as Mel, so she and Daisy nipped over the pooch course easily.

"Wow," whispered Amber. "I almost don't recognize Sam when she's not trying to control a frisky animal!"

Cara laughed. "It's weird! But they're wicked, aren't they?"

"Well good!" Mel answered. "Everybody

else is gonna have to work hard to be as fast as them. Maybe they'll be the ones to kick Henrietta's butt!"

It definitely looked like it. A few more contestants followed them. One boy did the course by himself – first with his lovely Highland pony and then with his border collie – and he was very fast too.

Vicki came up and watched with Mel and the girls while they waited for their turn. "He'll be a good show-jumper in a few years' time," she commented.

Mel wished that Vicki would say that about her one day. She was just imagining herself storming through the course at Badminton on Candy when Vicki's voice interrupted her thoughts. "OK, you two," she was saying to Jess and Amber. "I'll walk over with you. That was your numbers being called. Go get 'em!"

"Woo-hoo!" shouted Cara and Mel. "Go, Amber! Go, Jess!"

Amber started well. She wasn't as strong as Darcy and she was a bit nervous because she'd broken her arm last year and hadn't ridden for a while. But Mel and Cara cheered as she and Stella cleared the first two jumps easily.

They were approaching the next jump

when Mel and Cara heard a scream: "Ugh! Disgusting rat! Get away from me!"

"Uh-oh!" said Mel. "Sounds like trouble."

"Oh, no!" Cara cried. "Melly, I'm so sorry. I was concentrating on Am and not on Treasure. He was sitting down by my feet but now he's over by Henrietta and Camilla."

Cara and Mel legged it over to the two livery girls and Treasure, who was barking loudly. Lots of the other waiting contestants were laughing their heads off, while Henrietta shrieked loudly. The two stable girls got there just in time to catch Treasure weeing all over her riding boot! Henrietta was hopping around trying to get away from him, and Camilla was trying to shoo the puppy away!

Mel and Cara laughed their heads off.

"It's not funny," Camilla snapped, looking daggers at them. "Do something, you idiots!" All *she* was doing was making things worse and splashing more wee up Henrietta's leg!

"It *is* funny!" Mel whispered to Cara.

Finally Treasure finished weeing. Cara quickly scooped him up off the floor and kissed him on his little pink nose.

Henrietta looked as if she was about to

kill someone. "Don't kiss it!" she yelled at
Cara. "Get it away from me!"

"Don't worry," Mel shouted back at her,
stepping in between the livery girl and
Cara, who was shaking. "We're all going –

you smell a bit funny anyway, Henrietta!"
And she and Cara ran off, giggling.

They were laughing so hard that they
didn't hear their numbers being called.

Vicki came to find them. "You're up next.

Didn't you hear?"

"OK," said Mel, still laughing.

"What's so funny, girls?" asked Vicki.

Cara spotted a furious Henrietta storming towards them. "I think Henrietta will tell you, Vicki!" she told her.

"Uh-oh," Vicki said with a groan. "OK. I'll deal with this. Now off you go! Have lots of fun and *take it easy*, Mel."

The girls made their way to the start, just as the steward was about to call their numbers again.

"I'm sorry we're late," Mel told him politely, then turned to Cara. "We had a bit of a sticky situation!" she joked. Cara burst out laughing again.

Mel and Cara giggled their way round the whole course! Mel took her time, approaching the jumps carefully. After each one she stroked Candy's chestnut mane and whispered, "Well done, babe, you're doing brilliantly," and then grinned over at Cara.

Cara and Treasure were good too. Cara had trained the puppy well and he nipped over each jump perfectly. When their times had been recorded, Cara dropped down onto the grass, panting. "Good one, Treasure," she said, hugging the puppy.

Mel led Candy over to them. "Well done, guys!" she called. "You were wicked!"

"You were," Vicki said, coming over too. She scooped Treasure up and held him out in front of her. "Even though you're a very naughty boy for dirtying Henrietta's clean riding clothes." She turned to the girls and winked. "Henrietta couldn't *possibly* compete with wet jodhpurs, so unfortunately she and Camilla had to be driven back to the stables and missed the competition."

"What a shame!" Mel said, grinning.

"I do feel bad," Cara said, still red in the face. "I should have kept an eye on Treasure."

"Don't worry, babe," Vicki said comfortingly. "It was Henrietta's choice to leave. I offered to find her some other jodhpurs to wear but she didn't want them."

"That doesn't surprise me." Mel laughed. "They were probably *too common*!" she said, copying Henrietta's snooty voice.

"Well, it means that you were the last to compete, so we just need to wait for them to announce the winners and give out the medals." Vicki smiled. "Just chill out here for a bit."

Mel left Candy with Cara and went over to stand with her dad and Cathy while the prizes were given out. She whooped and cheered as Jess and Amber got third place. The boy on the Highland pony came second. Darcy and Sam won by miles!

"Go, Vicki's Riding School!" she called loudly, waving at her friends.

"You're not disappointed, are you, Mel?" asked her dad, putting his arm round her. "I know how competitive you are!"

Mel looked at him, then at Cathy, and then over at her friends, who were all smiling and waving at her, holding their medals up. "No, Dad. I'm not disappointed at all. I'm happy. Candy's well again and I'm the luckiest girl in the world," she said as she gave him and Cathy a big hug.